THE WISE MEN OF CHELM AND THE FOOLISH CARP

Green
Bean
Books

First published in the UK in 2020 by Green Bean Books
c/o Pen & Sword Books Ltd
47 Church Street, Barnsley, South Yorkshire, S70 2AS, England
www.greenbeanbooks.com

Paperback edition: 978-1-78438-565-1
Harold Grinspoon Foundation edition: 978-1-78438-569-9

Designed by Saray García Rúa
Edited by Kate Baker
Production by Hugh Allan

Printed in China by 1010 Printing International Ltd
092030K1/B1534/A7

FSC
www.fsc.org

MIX
Paper from
responsible sources
FSC® C016973

THE WISE MEN OF CHELM AND THE FOOLISH CARP

Witten by Isaac Bashevis Singer

Illustrated by Viktoria Efremova

IN the city of Chelm, every family bought fish for the Sabbath. The rich bought large fish, the poor, small ones. They were bought on Thursday, chopped and made into gefilte fish on Friday, and eaten on the Sabbath.

One Thursday morning, the door opened at the house of the community leader of Chelm, Gronam Ox, and Zeinvel Ninny entered, carrying a bucket full of water. Inside was a large, live carp.

"What is this?" Gronam asked.

"A gift to you from the wise men of Chelm," Zeinvel said. "This is the largest carp ever caught in the Lake of Chelm, and we all decided to give it to you as a token of appreciation for your great wisdom."

"Thank you very much," Gronam Ox replied. "My wife, Yente Pesha, will be delighted. She and I both love carp. I read in a book that eating the brain of a carp increases wisdom, and even though we in Chelm are immensely clever, a little improvement never hurts. But let me have a close look at him. I was told that a carp's tail shows the size of his brain."

Gronam Ox was known to be near-sighted, and when he bent down to the bucket to better observe the carp's tail, the carp did something that proved he was not as wise as Gronam thought. He lifted his tail and smacked Gronam across the face.

Gronam Ox was flabbergasted. "Nothing like this has ever happened to me before!" he exclaimed. "I cannot believe this carp was caught in the Chelm lake. A Chelm carp would know better."

"He's the meanest fish I've ever seen!" agreed Zeinvel Ninny.

Even though Chelm was a big city, news travelled quickly. In no time at all the other wise men of Chelm arrived at the house of their leader, Gronam Ox. Treitel Fool came, and Sender Donkey, and Shmendrick Numskull, and Dopey Lekisch.

Gronam Ox was saying, "I'm not going to eat this fish on the Sabbath. This carp is a fool, and malicious to boot. If I eat him, I could become foolish instead of more clever."

Gronam Ox put a finger to his head as a sign that he was thinking hard. After a while, he cried out, "No man or animal in Chelm should slap Gronam Ox! This fish should be punished."

"What kind of punishment shall we give him?" asked Treitel Fool. "He should be punished in a special way to show that no one can smack our beloved sage, Gronam Ox, and get away with it."

What kind of punishment?
wondered Shmendrick
Numskull. "Shall we
perhaps imprison him?"

"There is no prison in Chelm for fish,"
said Zeinvel Ninny. "And to build such a
prison would take too long."

"This case needs lengthy
consideration," Gronam Ox
decided. "Let's leave the carp in
the tub outside and ponder the
matter as long as is necessary. Being
the wisest man in Chelm, I cannot
afford to pass a sentence that will not
be admired by all Chelmites."

"If the carp stays in the tub for a long time, he may die," Zeinvel Ninny, a former fish dealer, explained. "To keep him alive, we will need to put him into an even larger tub, and the water has to be changed often. He must also be fed properly."

"You are right, Zeinvel," Gronam Ox told him. "Go and find the largest tub in Chelm and see to it that the carp is kept alive and healthy until the day of judgement. When I reach a decision, you will hear about it."

Of course, Gronam's words were the law in Chelm. The five wise men went and found a huge tub. They filled it with fresh water and put the criminal carp in it, together with some crumbs of challah and other tidbits a carp might like to eat. Shlemiel, Gronam's bodyguard, was stationed at the tub to make sure that no greedy Chelmite would use the imprisoned carp for gefilte fish.

It just so happened that Gronam Ox had many other decisions to make, and he kept postponing the sentence.

The carp seemed not to be impatient. He ate, swam in the tub, and became even fatter than he had been, not realizing that a severe sentence hung over his head.

Shlemiel changed the water frequently because he was told that if the carp died, this would be an act of contempt for Gronam Ox and for Chelm's Court of Justice. Yukel the water carrier made a few extra pennies every day by bringing water for the carp.

Some of the Chelmites, who were in opposition to Gronam Ox, spread the rumour that Gronam just couldn't find the right type of punishment and that he was waiting for the carp to die a natural death. But, as always, a great disappointment awaited them.

One morning, about half a year later, the sentence became known and when it was known, Chelm was stunned. The carp had to be drowned.

Gronam Ox had thought up many clever sentences before, but never one as brilliant as this one. Even his enemies were amazed at the shrewd verdict.

This was just the sort of punishment suited to a spiteful carp with a large tail and a small brain.

That day, the entire Chelm community
gathered at the lake to see the sentence carried out.

The carp, which had become
almost twice as big as he had been before,
was brought to the lake in the wagon
that took criminals to prison.

Drummers drummed. Trumpeters trumpeted.
The Chelmite Chief Justice raised the heavy carp
and threw it into the lake with a mighty splash.

A great cry rose from the Chelmites:
"Down with the treacherous carp!
Long live Gronam Ox!
Hurrah!"

Gronam was lifted by his admirers
and carried home with songs of praise.

Some Chelmites showered him
with flowers. Even Yente Pesha, his wife, who was often
critical of Gronam and dared to call him foolish,
seemed impressed by Gronam's high intelligence.

Just the same, to be on the safe side, the wise men of Chelm published a decree stating that if the nasty carp refused to be drowned and was caught again, then a special jail should be built for him. It would be a pool where he would be kept for the rest of his life.

The decree was printed in capital letters in the official newspaper of Chelm and signed by Gronam Ox and his five sages – Treitel Fool, Sender Donkey, Shmendrick Numskull, Zeinvel Ninny, and Dopey Lekisch.